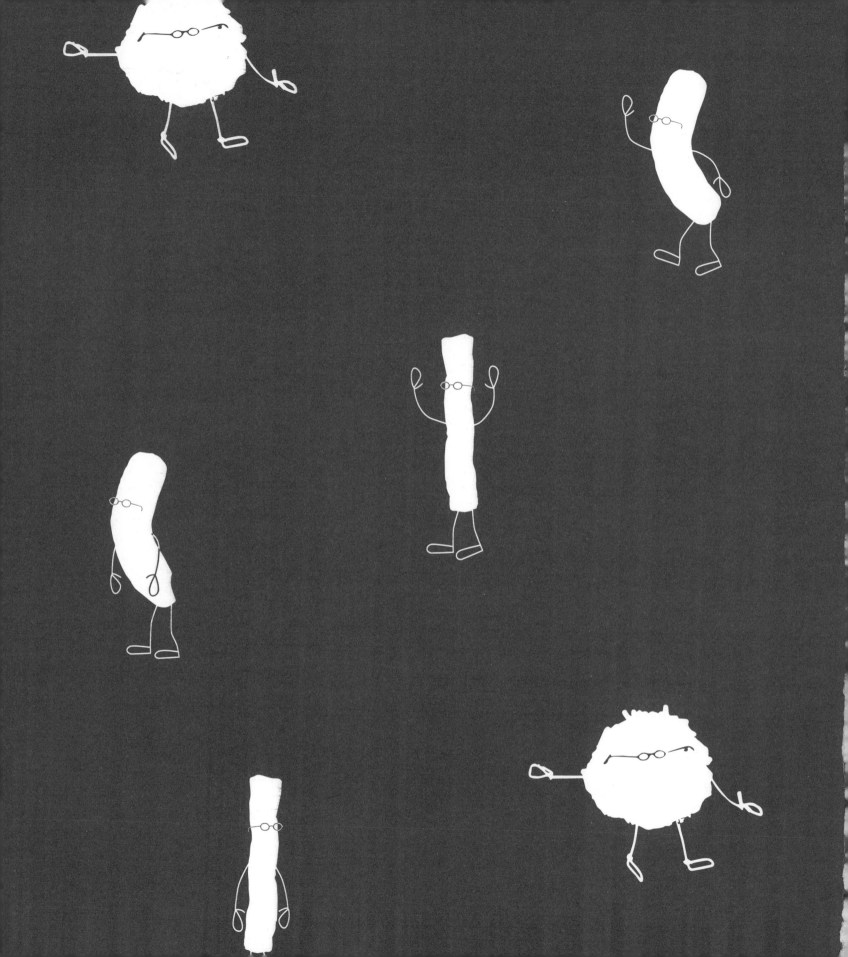

SCAREDY SNACKS!

TERRY BORDER

PHILOMEL BOOKS

PHILOMEL BOOKS

An imprint of Penguin Random House LLC
New York

First published in the United States of America by Philomel,
an imprint of Penguin Random House LLC, 2020.

Visit us online at penguinrandomhouse.com

Library of Congress Cataloging-in-Publication Data is available.

Manufactured in China
ISBN 9781524740160
10 9 8 7 6 5 4 3 2 1

Edited by Jill Santopolo.
Design by Ellice M. Lee.
Text set in Hank BT.
The art was done by manipulating and photographing three-dimensional objects.

To Judi,
my partner in this adventure
of a life. Where do you want
to go next, my dear?

It was cleaning day at the snack cabinet, and everyone was hard at work.

But Sprinkles didn't feel like cleaning at all. Instead, she wanted to welcome Dr. Nuttenstein, the new neighbor who had moved in next door. Word on the kitchen counter was that he was a little . . . bananas.

But Sprinkles didn't care—she was
a tough cookie—and convinced her friends
Doodle and Pretzel to come along.

Dr. Nuttenstein
Mad Scientist

One of the doors to the creepy old house wasn't quite closed, and when they knocked it swung wide open.

Creeeeeak!

"Hello?" called Sprinkles. "Is anybody home?"

All they heard was silence. Sprinkles stopped to think.

"Let's just put our welcome card inside," she said.

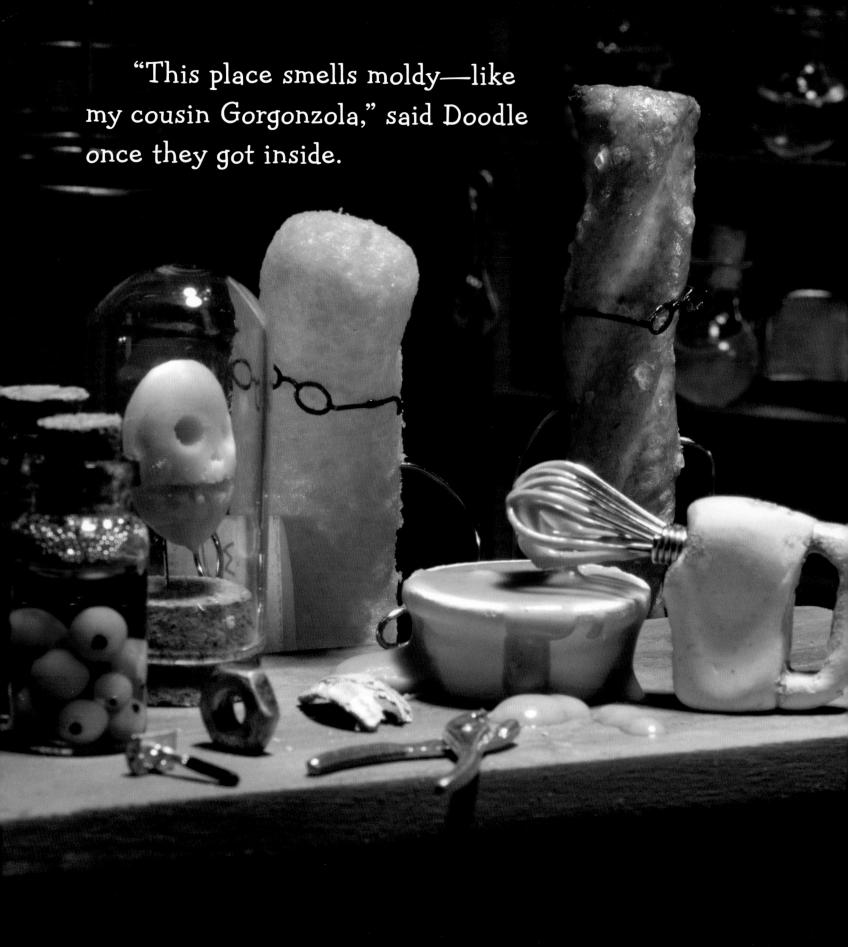

"This place smells moldy—like my cousin Gorgonzola," said Doodle once they got inside.

"It's twisted," said Pretzel, "and not in a good way. This Dr. Nuttenstein seems rotten."

"Aw, stop acting like baby food," said Sprinkles. Then they heard the door again.

Creeeeeak!

Someone was coming!

"That must be Dr. Nuttenstein!"
whispered Pretzel.

"I think that's what a mad scientist looks like!" whispered Cheese Doodle.
Sprinkles didn't say anything.

They watched as Dr. Nuttenstein used
blenders and choppers.
He pushed buttons. He flipped switches.
And then, a loud ZAAAP!!!

"It's ALIVE!" shouted Dr. Nuttenstein.

The three friends realized that they were in a terrible pickle.

"It's a monster cookie!" whispered Pretzel.

"A cookie monster!" moaned Doodle.

"A peanut butter biscuit beast!" gasped Sprinkles.

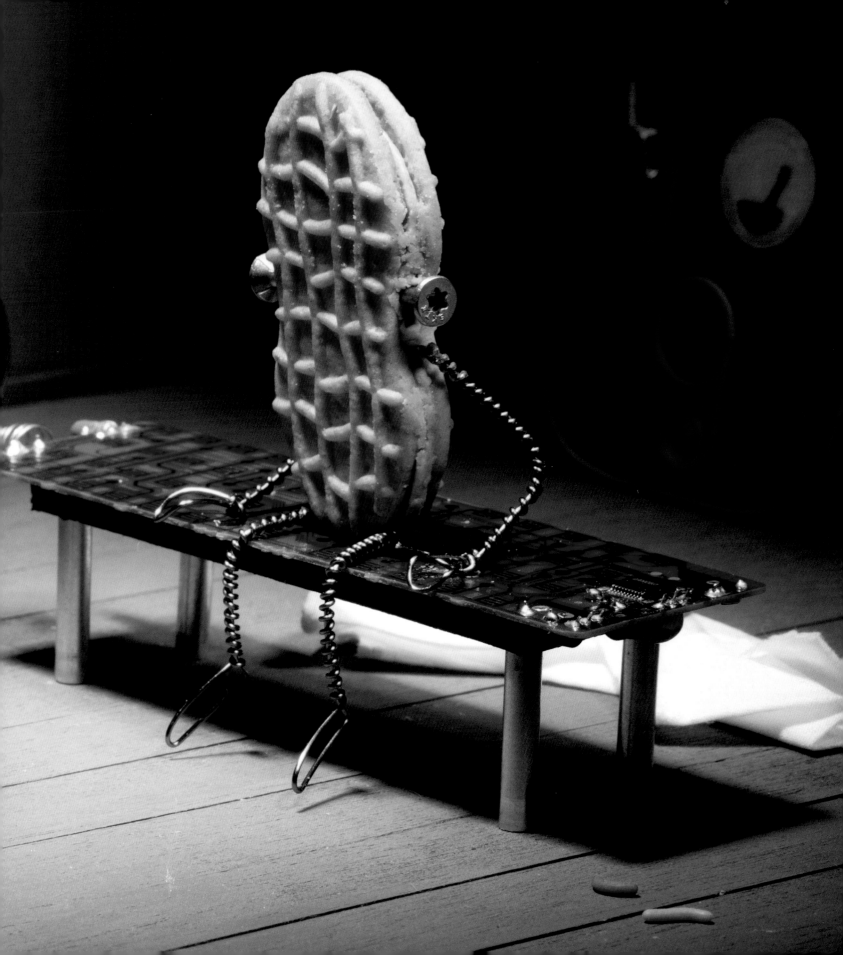

Just then, Dr. Nuttenstein looked
down at the floor.

"Who made this mess?" he asked
his cookie creation. "We'll have to
teach them a lesson."

"That nutty doctor is going to find us!" whispered Cheese Doodle. "He could turn me into a grilled cheese doodle."

"I feel like crying!" sobbed Pretzel, "and then I'll be soggy."

"A-HA!"

Dr. Nuttenstein shouted.

The trio froze like Popsicles.
The doctor studied them carefully
and then, slowly and quietly, said,
"Come with me."

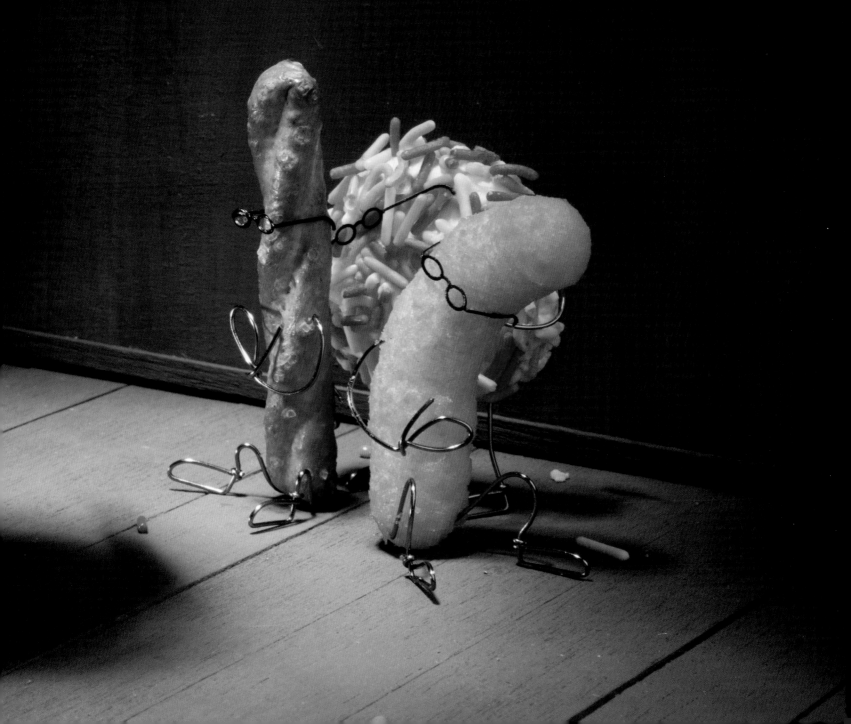

He searched through his gruesome tools.
Sprinkles and her friends were horrified. They were
petrified! They were dizzy with fear!

Then Dr. Nuttenstein spoke his
nightmarish words . . .

"Take these brooms and get busy!" he said. "I want this place spotless."

"Oh no!" cried the snacks.

But as they cleaned, they found out that if they worked together it wasn't so bad. So when Sprinkles took a break and didn't come back,

Doodle and Pretzel were pretty upset.
They went home to let her know.

Dr. Nutten
Mad ...er

After waving goodbye to
the snacks, Dr. Nuttenstein and
his creature friend got ready for
dinner. But it turned out that the
creature wasn't hungry at all.

Because sometimes, that's
the way the cookie crumbles.

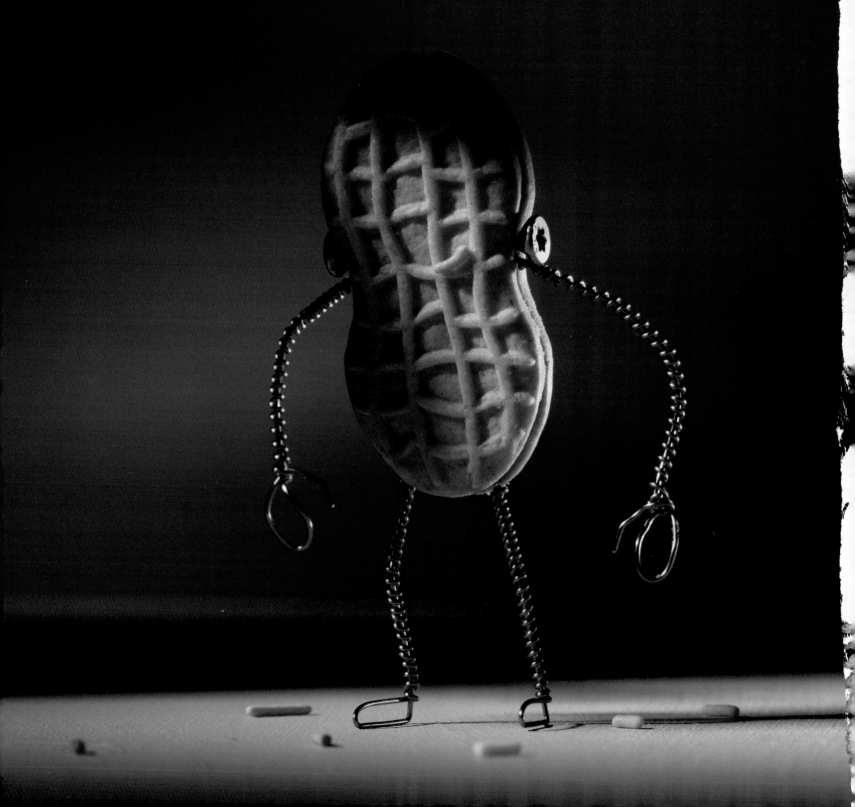